2015 Christmas

This Book Belongs
to

Helzer Children

Sweet Pea & Friends
The SheepOver

Sweet Pea Press
15 Gray Way
Essex Junction, Vermont 05452
www.mysweetpeapress.com
inquiries@mysweetpeapress.com
802.899.2000

Printed in the United States of America
Published in Vermont, USA

Published by Sweet Pea Press
First Edition Printing, 2015

ISBN 978-0-578-16599-8

Library of Congress Control Number: 2015910152

Publisher's Cataloging-in-Publication Data

Churchman, John, 1957- author, illustrator.
    Sweet Pea & friends : the sheepOver / story by John and Jennifer Churchman ; photo illustrations by John Churchman.—First edition.
    pages cm
    LCCN 2015910152
    SUMMARY: This photo-illustrated book is the story of an orphan lamb, Sweet Pea, who lives on a farm in Vermont. When she becomes ill, she recovers with the help of the farmer, the vet and her farmyard friends.
    Audience: Ages 0-12.
    ISBN 978-0-578-16599-8

    1. Lambs—Juvenile fiction. 2. Domestic animals—Juvenile fiction. 3. Health—Juvenile fiction.
    4. Friendship—Juvenile fiction. [1. Sheep—Fiction.
    2. Domestic animals—Fiction. 3. Health—Fiction.
    4. Friendship—Fiction.]   I. Churchman, Jennifer, author.
    II. Title. III. Title: Sweet Pea and friends.

    PZ7.1.C48Swe 2015   [E]
            QBI15-600136

Sweet Pea & Friends
The SheepOver

Story by John and Jennifer Churchman

Photo Illustrations by John Churchman

Sweet Pea Press

Essex, Vermont

It was way past bedtime,
and Laddie the sheep dog
was still awake.

The winter moon hung low
in the sky, and Laddie heard
Owl calling from the forest,
whooo, whoo, whoooo.

Laddie woke Farmer John
with a gentle nudge.
Something was not right
in the barn . . .

Wild Red Fox moved swiftly past on silent, snowy paws. He glanced at the farmer and his sheepdog as they headed to the barn, then faded into the night.

All was silent in the barn
as Laddie moved quietly
past Sadie the pony and
around the watching sheep.

He found Sweet Pea, the orphan lamb, curled on the hay. Her closest friends Prem, Sunny, and Violet stood nearby, urging her "Up, up, up."

Sweet Pea's nose was hot and pink. She could not stand up by herself, so Farmer John gently lifted her and started up the hill to the greenhouse.

Buff Orpington the rooster stirred as the farmer walked past. Then he crowed loudly, "Sweet Pea, Sweet Pea! Something's wrong with Sweet Pea!"

Keeper the goose startled
awake and took flight, honking
"Sweet Pea, Sweet Pea—
What's wrong with Sweet Pea?"

Farmer John placed Sweet Pea
on the soft, dry hay in the
warm greenhouse and called
Vet Alison, a country veternarian
who traveled from farm to farm,
taking care of animals.

She carefully examined Sweet Pea, who had an injured leg and a fever. Vet Alison gave her medicine to help her feel better.

"Keep Sweet Pea quiet, and have her rest. She will also need a friend for company," Vet Alison told Farmer John.

Farmer John brought Sweet Pea's
good friend Prem to stay with her
so she wouldn't feel lonely.

Sweet Pea looked forward to getting better. Vet Alison had told her that when she was well again and could walk down the hill to the barn, she could have a sleep over in the greenhouse with her friends to celebrate.

The day finally came when Sweet Pea felt able to walk down the hill to the barn for her appointment with Vet Allison. Her friends Sunny and Violet were there to welcome her.

Vet Alison gave Sweet Pea a final check-up and declared, "Sweet Pea is much better!"

Now that she was well, Sweet Pea invited
her friends to come that very evening
to the greenhouse for a SheepOver Party.

Farm dogs Cyrie, Quinn, and Laddie
heard the good news and ran through
the farmyard, barking "Sweet Pea is better!
Sweet Pea is better!"

It was all the talk
of the henhouse:
Sweet Pea was
feeling better!

The ducks quacked happily to each other and told their friend Tom, the big bronze turkey, "Sweet Pea is better now!"

Midsummer the farm cat, purring loudly, asked his friend Tom, "Did I hear Sweet Pea is feeling better?"

"Yes, yes," gobbled Tom.
"Sweet Pea is better.
Sweet Pea is better!"

Sweet Pea could hardly wait for her friends
to arrive for her SheepOver Party. Sadie the pony
helped Sunny and Violet get ready.

Farmer John and Laddie came to lead
Sweet Pea's friends to the SheepOver.

First Violet arrived, and then
Sunny, who was so excited
that she jumped for joy.

The farmer's wife, Jennifer, had made
colorful trays of their favorite treats: pumpkin
slices for Sunny, sweet beets for Violet,
and for Sweet Pea, the tender tips of
pine-tree branches. Prem gladly
tasted everything.

There were apples, too, and oats sprinkled on top. Everyone enjoyed the feast and ended up with pumpkin-stained faces.

"What should we do now?"
asked Violet, licking the last
of the pumpkin from her lips.

"Let's dress up like Farmer John," Sunny cried, giving the farmer's hat a toss in the air. The friends all took turns trying on Farmer John's hat, which he had left by the greenhouse door.

"Let's dance now," Sunny said as she started the music for dancing under the disco ball.

Just then, Laddie was passing by. He poked his head through an open windowpane. "A disco ball!" he exclaimed. He had never seen such a thing in the farmer's greenhouse.

After dancing, everyone was very tired. It was now Sweet Pea's turn to choose what they did next before bedtime.

"Let's have Farmer John read us the story about Uncle Ollie when he was a little orphan lamb on the farm," she said.

"Yes!" they all cried, for that story was their favorite.

After the story, Farmer John turned out the greenhouse lights and wished them all goodnight.

As the four friends snuggled down in the soft hay to sleep, Sweet Pea felt very happy to be better and back with her friends.

This was the best SheepOver ever,
Sweet Pea thought as she and her
friends drifted off to sleep.

Dedicated with love to our children
Kailie, Travis, and Gabrielle

We are eternally grateful to all of our family, friends, and online community for their loving and generous encouragement, feedback, and support along the way. We would like to give special thanks to editor C. Carol Halitsky for her caring attention to detail, typography consultant Donda Thibault for finding the perfect fonts with which to present our story, and DVM Alison Cornwall for the care and expertise that saved Sweet Pea's life.

Sweet Pea & Friends: The SheepOver is award-winning photographer John Churchman's debut children's book. Drawing on his talents as an artist, photographer, and farmer, he brings this story to life, with his enchanting photo-illustrations.

Jennifer Churchman, a multimedia artist and business consultant, has loved telling and writing stories all her life. Her professional career also includes helping clients communicate and develop their own brand though authentic storytelling and visual elements that encourage engagement with their audience.

John and Jennifer bring their talents together to give voice to the stories of the animals that surround them and add boundless enjoyment to their lives. They have made their home on a small farm in the beautiful countryside of Essex, Vermont, with their daughter Gabrielle.

They are currently working on their next children's book and a variety of related creative projects, including an interactive website that continues the day-to-day story of Sweet Pea & Friends.

Beyond the Book . . .